3,95

S.

Catherine Brett

The
Women's
·Press·

Thanks to Kathy.
Special thanks to Ann and Heather.

Canadian Cataloguing in Publication Data

Brett, Catherine
S.P. likes A.D.

ISBN 0-88961-142-4

I. Title.

PS8553.R486S2 1989   jC813'.54   C89-094952-2
PZ7.B747Sp 1989

Cover art: Dianne Hunt
Cover design: Christine Higdon
Editor: Ann Decter
Copy editor and proofreader: Ramabai Espinet

Published by The Women's Press
229 College Street, No. 204 Toronto, Ontario M5T 1R4

This book was produced by the collective
effort of members of The Women's Press.
This book was a project of the Young Readers Group.
Printed and bound in Canada.   GCUI

The Women's Press gratefully acknowledges financial support
from The Canada Council, the Ontario Arts Council and the
Lesbian and Gay Community Appeal.

For Gill

CHAPTER ONE

School always seemed busier on a Monday. It was livelier – more talking and jostling in the halls, more excitement. Everyone, refreshed and rejuvenated from the weekend, seemed to possess more energy and vitality on a Monday than on a Friday.

Stephanie made her way to her first class of the day – Math. Stephanie had trouble with Math, not because she didn't like it but because she couldn't do it. In fact she liked numbers a lot, the way they looked all neatly lined up in columns, the shape of the numbers themselves. She just didn't care much about what they meant when they were forced together in various mathematical contortions.

Taking her usual seat near the back of the class she spread her books out on the top of her desk and waited for the teacher to arrive and the class to begin.

"Wait till I tell you what I just found out." Stephanie's friend Devi slid into the seat beside her. "It's incredible." Devi tended towards the dramatic, sometimes to the point of embarrassment.

"Well?"

"I heard this morning. Lisa told me." Devi opened her math text and began slowly, almost lazily, turning the pages.

She always did this, always took forever to say what she apparently couldn't wait to say. And it always got Stephanie annoyed.

"Well?" she said again, a little sharply.

At that moment the teacher, Ms. Simpson, walked into the classroom and shut the door. Talking to Devi would now be difficult as Ms. Simpson didn't tolerate any noise apart from her own boring, droning voice. Stephanie felt herself getting more annoyed and shot a dangerous glance at Devi who looked back knowingly. Stephanie decided that if they hadn't known each other for such a long time she could easily stop being friends with Devi. It seemed sometimes that the longer you knew someone the more annoying they became.

"Page 45 please," said Ms. Simpson.

"Guess who likes you?" hissed Devi.

"Who?" said Stephanie, too loudly.

"Quiet please," said Ms. Simpson, "and turn to page 45, exercise 4.6."

"Who?"

Devi would have liked to draw the suspense out

for another ten minutes but the fact that talking was difficult, if not dangerous, was spoiling her plans. She even looked a little annoyed herself, Stephanie thought.

"Who?"

"Eric Sullivan."

"Eric Sullivan?"

"That's what I said."

"Stephanie and Devi, would you please be quiet. This isn't a place for socializing."

Eric Sullivan was in Stephanie's history class. A nice guy. Fairly good looking. Funny. But from what Stephanie could tell he didn't seem to be particularly interested in her.

"Are you sure?"

Devi leaned over towards Stephanie to avoid detection from Ms. Simpson.

"Lisa told me and Lisa should know."

Stephanie wasn't sure why Lisa should know or why Devi seemed to have absolute confidence in what Lisa should know. But, it could be true. Maybe it was true. There were worse people to be liked by than Eric Sullivan. The problem was that Stephanie didn't like Eric Sullivan back. He was a nice guy and she thought he was quite smart and funny and she did like him, but not in *that* way.

7

"Isn't it great!" Devi's eager face was again leaning over towards Stephanie. From that comment Stephanie figured out two things: 1) That anyone (anyone being Stephanie) would be crazy not to like Eric Sullivan, as he was so wonderful; because 2) Devi liked Eric Sullivan.

Well, Stephanie didn't like him. The problem with Eric and with other boys who had liked her was that Stephanie didn't feel anything towards them. Nothing. Zero.

There was someone, though, who made Stephanie's heart beat so fast she thought it might stop. Someone whom, since the beginning of the school year, Stephanie had worshipped. She wondered what Devi would say if she told her who she did like. She almost felt like doing it, like leaning over conspiratorially towards her friend and whispering: "I don't like Eric Sullivan – I like Anne Delaney."

Anne Delaney was in Stephanie's history class too. And in her English class. From the first moment Stephanie had seen her she'd liked her. It was crazy really: to have such a strong feeling for someone she'd barely spoken to. And for a girl. It was crazy and incredibly confusing.

Stephanie had never felt this way about anyone

before, a feeling so powerful she wasn't sure she knew what it was. How could she know if she'd never felt it before? She tried to make a list of "Reasons why I like Anne Delaney" but only put down "I don't know" seventeen times. All Stephanie did know was that the feeling was bigger than she was and stronger than she was and couldn't be controlled. No matter how hard she tried not to think about Anne Delaney she only ended up thinking about her harder. She wasn't doing very well in English and History because she spent the entire time watching Anne Delaney.

Stephanie lived in fear that one day Anne Delaney might speak to her and that she wouldn't be able to reply, or worse, that she'd say something stupid, so stupid that it was beyond stupid. Luckily Anne Delaney hadn't ever said anything to her. Nothing, in four and a half months. Not one word. Why not?

Stephanie looked down at her closed text book and realized that she wasn't listening to a thing Ms. Simpson was saying. Thinking about Anne Delaney was dangerous. It made her whole world stop. The only thing that made her quit thinking about Anne Delaney was when she thought about bones and paleontology. Perhaps her feeling for bones was stronger than her feeling for Anne Delaney. Or maybe it just required more concentration. Stephanie drew a femur on the cover of her binder. It didn't make her feel any better.

The worst part was that when she thought about Anne Delaney it was really quite boring. In her thoughts Anne Delaney was just – well – there. She wasn't doing anything or saying anything. She was just standing around. Once she'd been sitting at a table. Stephanie had tried to make Anne Delaney do things in her thoughts but it didn't work. She would just stand there, looking kind of fed up. Stephanie had also tried to put herself with Anne Delaney in her thoughts but the moment she could visualize herself she could no longer visualize Anne Delaney and she was left standing there, alone and confused.

Stephanie drew the shoulder blade of a horse.

"Quiz," hissed Devi, and yes, it was true, Ms. Simpson was starting to write questions on the blackboard. Stephanie groaned. Sometimes it seemed that everything was completely unfair.

CHAPTER TWO

When Stephanie left school it was snowing. There was nothing but snow these days and winter was only half over. Luckily this was the kind of snowing Stephanie liked – large, heavy flakes that slid lazily down from the sky. Not the kind of snowing that came slanting out of a sharp wind and stung your cheeks and eyes.

Stephanie was walking slowly towards home, wondering why her friends were such cowards and had taken the bus. She had wrapped her school books in a plastic bag to save them from getting wet and clutched it against her chest. Snow made the world go quiet and solemn which she liked. She liked that the snow could darken the city and that the street lights had to come on to cleave a path through the whiteness.

She was walking along, thinking about how much she liked snow when she suddenly saw her. Anne Delaney. Up ahead by the mailbox. Immediately Stephanie felt like hiding and found herself looking frantically around for something to crouch behind. "Don't be stupid" she said to herself. "You don't need to hide. Even if she turned around, through this snow she'd never be able to see who it was. And even if she did see who it was she wouldn't think anything of it."

Anne Delaney. Stephanie strained her eyes through the thickening whiteness to discern every movement. She should have known that Anne Delaney was no coward, that Anne Delaney would never have been forced by a little snow to take the bus home. Stephanie wondered where Anne lived. She'd never seen her walking home before, even though she'd been secretly hoping to since the beginning of school. Anne Delaney turned the corner by the mailbox and Stephanie hurried forward through the snow so she wouldn't lose sight of her. She was a good three hundred yards behind Anne Delaney and she stayed close to telephone poles and street lights – just in case. Anne Delaney wasn't moving very quickly. Perhaps she liked this kind of snow too and was enjoying being out in it. Or perhaps she was just a slow walker.

Stephanie had never told anyone about her attraction to Anne Delaney. For one thing, she didn't know for sure what it was she was feeling. For another, she knew, that no one would really understand. If she had liked Eric Sullivan she would have been able to tell the whole world and the whole world would have been pleased. But this was a different thing altogether. It was alright to tell people that you preferred strawberry ice-cream to chocolate when they all liked chocolate better. It was quite another thing to tell your friends that you liked a girl.

Stephanie remembered in Grade 1 when two girls had held hands during recess and some of the other kids had yelled "Lezzies, lezzies." No one, probably not even the kids doing the shouting, knew what "lezzie" meant. But they had all known it was an insult to be called that. They all thought it was something bad. Anytime Stephanie had heard the term "lesbian" or "dyke" or "homosexual" it had always been in a negative context. Once, as a child, she'd been with her family in a park and there were two women walking over the grass with their arms around each other. Her father had said, "Look at those dykes," his voice hard. It sounded like, "Look at those freaks." He'd acted as if they were not just different, but sick, evil.

Stephanie knew that lesbians were women who were sexually attracted to other women, but if she liked Anne Delaney, did this make her a lesbian?

What did it make her? Anything? Her attraction to Anne Delaney was not something she felt she could control. It had just – well – happened and there was nothing that could be done about it. Why did that have to be a bad thing? Maybe it wasn't a bad thing. But if that was the case then why did people think that it was?

Anne Delaney had crossed the street and turned another corner. Stephanie crossed the street as well and suddenly realized that she was no longer walking home. She was following Anne Delaney home. Why? Another question she didn't have an answer for. It seemed that a lot of what Stephanie did these days was done because *she had to do it*. She didn't feel like she had any choice. It felt like she lived by emotions. By a feeling, a strong feeling.

Anne Delaney stopped suddenly and turned around and Stephanie hurled herself into a snowbank. What if she knew she was being followed? What would she think? What did it mean? *What did it mean?* What did anything mean? Stephanie lay face down in the snow, arms outstretched at her sides and thought about these questions. They were very good questions. What they needed were very good answers to go with them. Stephanie felt her face begin to freeze from the snow grating against it and stood up, feeling a little shaky. Anne Delaney had started walking again and was a lot further ahead and Stephanie had to run to close the distance between them.

Anne Delaney looked back several more times and each time Stephanie had to leap in a frantic and dangerous manner out of sight. Once she even threw herself through a hedge and continued following with small twigs embedded in her snow-encrusted hair. She was beginning to get annoyed with Anne Delaney. Why did she have to keep looking back? And why wasn't she home yet? She seemed to live about three times as far from the school as Stephanie. Why, if she did live so far away, did she walk home? Why couldn't she take the bus, like a normal sensible person would? Stephanie stopped walking. It was a crazy thing to do, trailing behind, following, and she didn't even know why she was doing it. So why keep on? Stephanie decided to give up. Anne Delaney crossed another street. Stephanie decided she'd come too far to give up and hurried to cross the street as well.

Then suddenly it was over. Anne Delaney had walked up the driveway of a grey highrise and had disappeared through the front door. Stephanie stood beside a telephone pole and felt her feet grow cold in the snow. Now what? So she knew where Anne Delaney lived. So what?

Maybe she would crawl through the snow to the lobby and raise herself weakly up to buzz the apartment. And when Anne Delaney answered the intercom she would explain, slowly (due to the numbness in her body and voice) that she was dying from the cold and that she had managed to make it to here but could go no further. And perhaps Anne Delaney would rush downstairs and take her inside and make her something hot to drink and talk to her about her courage and her near-death experience and let Stephanie stay in the house with her for – forever.

Stephanie sniffed loudly and fumbled with a stiff hand in her coat pocket for a tissue. She stamped her feet several times to shake the cold out of them, then she turned around and slowly began her trek home.

CHAPTER THREE

Stephanie was up in her room making a list of all the things she had to have done by the end of the month. She was already on her second page.

From downstairs she could hear her brother Mark calling out to either or both of her parents for various possessions he'd managed to misplace over the course of his lifetime. Mark was moving into residence at his university and was frantically trying to round up everything he owned in one week. He had to start back on January 8th.

"Fishing rod," he bellowed from one floor down.

"Fishing rod?" replied her mother's incredulous voice. "You haven't fished since you were ten. When's the last time you even thought about fishing?"

"Where is it?"

"I gave it away."

"You gave it away!"

Stephanie knew she would miss her brother. He was practically her best friend and they'd never been apart for any great length of time. When he couldn't get into residence in September she thought she'd have him around for another year and was secretly glad. When a place opened up for the beginning of second term she felt cheated somehow. She knew she'd miss him – but later. Right now she just wanted him to shut up. She doodled a fishing rod in the margin of her page.

Stephanie wasn't supposed to be making lists. She was supposed to be filling out the application for her high school art contest. But it was a long application and she'd been trying to think of the dimensions of her project and that had made her think of something else. She'd forgotten about dimensions altogether and had started on a list. It was easier to make a list of things to be done than to actually start doing them. Anyway, she didn't expect she'd even get an honourable mention. The competition was open to everyone in her high school, and she, only in Grade 9, had to compete against the higher grades.

Still … her art teacher had been impressed with her project idea. The art contest was for a sculpture to be erected on the grounds at the front of the school. The winner received money to cover all building expenses and had her name engraved on a plaque at the base of the sculpture. Stephanie's project was an abstract piece that relied upon the juxtaposition of various shapes. What made her idea different was that her sculpture would be made of replicated dinosaur bones from different dinosaurs. The bones would be arranged to form a huge dinosaur head. Rib bones would be used for the shape of the head itself. A pelvic bone would be the skull plate. The jaws would be formed from leg bones and the teeth from the spine plates of a Stegosaurus. The bones would be made (to exact dimensions) in plaster and then cast in concrete.

Stephanie was entering the art contest chiefly because of her interest in dinosaurs. She was interested in bones, period. She wanted to be a paleontologist. She was pleased with her idea for the sculpture because, after all, when paleontologists found dinosaur bones they didn't find them all connected properly in a dinosaur shape. They found them in clusters and clumps, much like her proposed sculpture.

"Goalie pads," Mark yelled. Stephanie wondered why Mark was taking such an interest in sports equipment he'd last used when he was ten. Maybe he thought that transporting all his junk to the residence would make him feel more at home. She put down her list and picked up the application form again. "Dimensions." Large. No, they didn't want large, they wanted numbers. Twelve feet. It was the first dimension that came into her head. Under "height" she wrote down "twelve feet."

The deadline for the competition application was Tuesday morning at 9:00 a.m. Today was Monday. Monday evening. There were still two pages of questions that seemed to require hours of thought and then she had to draw sketches of the finished sculpture. Stephanie figured she'd still be filling out the application by 9:00 a.m. tomorrow. It seemed that no matter how far head she started projects she finished them only minutes before they were due. Maybe she spent too long making lists. Something was obviously not quite right with the way she worked.

There were so many projects to be done these days. Grade 9 was a lot harder than any of the previous grades. Stephanie was in a new school and this was both unsettling and exciting. Last year when she'd been in a senior public, the school had been small and cozy and she'd known practically everyone. High school was different – large and busy. Even though she'd been there an entire term she still wasn't sure she knew her way around. She didn't feel she "belonged" to her school. She still got lost sometimes. Everyone seemed so much older. She still had most of her friends from Grade 9 but they weren't in all her classes and she found herself surrounded by kids she didn't know. Being shy she didn't make friends easily and there were lots of people in her classes that she'd never said anything to. High school was a little overwhelming.

Mark seemed to have stopped shouting for his possessions and the house was suddenly and unnaturally quiet. Stephanie looked at the next question on the application form. "Dimensions." Again dimensions. More dimensions. What did they want? She'd had trouble enough even coming up with one dimension. It was too much for them to expect that she know exactly what she was going to do. People who wrote forms, she decided, just didn't understand the people who had to fill them out. Stephanie wondered if there were people who did nothing but write forms. Form writers who sat at a desk all day thinking up questions like: "Purpose of project?" and "Expected date of completion?" It was a horrifying prospect. "Purpose of project?" How could she possibly answer that? In the small space provided on the form Stephanie wrote down, "Does it need one?"

CHAPTER FOUR

Stephanie went into Mark's room and found him standing by his bed staring at his shelves. He didn't acknowledge her entrance. Perhaps he hadn't even noticed. She walked across the room, stepping carefully around piles of clothes on the floor and stood beside him.

"What are we looking at?"

"My stuff." Mark sighed and glanced over at his sister. "I seem to have more stuff than I remember having. I can't decide what to take and what to leave behind. Where did it all come from?" He sounded genuinely surprised that he had, in his eighteen years on earth, managed to acquire anything.

They both stared at the shelves again. Books and games and boxes and records, hoarded since childhood, were crammed into every available space on the floor to ceiling shelf unit.

Stephanie sat down heavily on the edge of the bed.

"I wish you weren't going." She flopped backwards, put her hands behind her head and scanned the ceiling. "Can I have your book on the planets?"

"Maybe."

"How about the one on ocean life?"

"I don't know." Mark reached up and pulled a box down from the top shelf. "My room in the residence is even smaller than this one," he said disgustedly. "I'll be lucky if I can take anything." He put the box on the bed and removed the lid. "You always had the biggest room."

"Well I didn't ask to have the biggest room."

"But you got it."

There was silence as they both contemplated the truth of this.

Stephanie rolled onto her side and propped herself up on an elbow to see what her brother was doing. Mark was assembling a plastic castle. It had been his favourite childhood toy.

"Why did you go to university if you don't know what you want to do?"

"What would I do if I didn't go?" Mark had erected one wall and a tower. "Maybe I'll find out now I'm there. It's hard not knowing what to do with your life." He snapped together another tower. "You're lucky. You have your bones."

Stephanie didn't say anything. At the moment,

with everything that had been going on having her "bones" was no comfort at all.

"Well," she said after a while, "being able to get along wonderfully with dead things isn't really that great. In fact," she added, "there are lots of times when I'd trade it for getting along better with living things." She watched Mark trying to secure the drawbridge to the castle wall.

"People."

"What people?"

"Just people."

Mark stood up from where he'd been kneeling on the floor and scrambled through his shelves.

"What are you looking for?"

"The knights. Don't you remember how this stupid drawbridge never worked right and I'd have to prop it closed by standing the black knight against it."

"In the moat."

"Right, the moat. I've forgotten the moat." More frantic rifling through boxes. The moat was a large plastic sheet with a circle of blue printed on it. In the finale of particularly vicious games of "the castle" all the knights and horses would be spectacularly arranged around this blue ring – lying in various positions of untimely demise.

"Mark?"

"Uh huh." Mark had managed to find both the moat and the knights and was spreading the plastic moat sheet across the bed.

"I have to tell you about this really dumb thing I did today."

"Ok." Mark looked at her over the moat. "Is it an interesting dumb thing?"

"It's just a dumb thing." Stephanie started picking through the box of knights. She was looking for her favourite one – the one with the white horse and the red lance.

"But the thing the dumb thing is a part of isn't a dumb thing." Stephanie was finding this a lot harder than she'd thought, even though she'd rehearsed it a hundred times in her mind.

"So what did you do?"

Stephanie rolled onto her back again and addressed the ceiling.

"I followed someone home from school."

"Why?"

This was a very good question. Stephanie held the plastic knight in both hands over her face and studied the underside of the horse. There was a line down the belly to indicate where the figure had been lifted from the mold. There were also lines on the soles of the knights' shoes. Or were they boots? Or were they just feet?

"I had to," she said savagely, deciding they were boots.

"Why?"

"I had to find out where they lived."

"They? I thought you said you followed someone?" Mark looked over at her in confusion. "How many people did you follow home?"

"One. A person." Stephanie leaned over and put the knight in the moat. "Anne." It sounded strange to say it out loud, this name that she'd been creeping through her mind for weeks. Spoken it almost didn't sound like it was the right name.

"And it wasn't easy." Stephanie sat up. "She looked back a couple of times and I had to sort of leap quickly behind poles and trees. And there aren't enough really large trees on the way to her house. Have you noticed that there aren't many large trees anywhere anymore. What happened to large trees?" She stopped suddenly and Mark wasn't sure if he should answer her or not – but he'd never thought about it and didn't really know – and he was just about to invent some answer when she started talking again.

"And she lives miles away. Miles. I don't know

how she has enough energy to make it back and forth to school everyday. I got a blister on my heel on the way home." Stephanie moved her knight with the red lance out of the moat and onto the green part of the plastic sheet. This wasn't easy. She felt so full of frustrations sometimes she couldn't keep quiet about this anymore. She had to tell someone about Anne Delaney. And Mark was the person she was closest to: the one she'd always told everything to first. She wanted to let him know what was going on. It was as if by following Anne home she felt like she had finally managed to *do* something about the feeling that overpowered her – even if it was a pretty silly thing to do. Now that she'd done something she wanted to tell someone. But it wasn't easy. She wasn't sure that Mark would understand, or that she'd be able to explain it properly. Or even that she understood.

"Why?" asked Mark.

"I don't know." Stephanie told the truth. But Mark didn't seem too concerned. In fact most of his attention was focused on the completion of the castle assembly.

No. She couldn't tell him. Maybe if there came a point when she could explain it better he'd be the one to tell. But not this time.

"What are you going to do with the castle now?" she asked.

"Nothing. I thought I might put together the farm next."

"Are you going to play with all your old toys?"

"Maybe." Mark was up and rummaging through his shelves again. "It's sort of like saying goodbye."

Stephanie knew what this was like. She'd been sort of saying goodbye to Mark for months. She moved towards the door.

"I'd better go and start my homework. When you get to the battleship game, come and get me."

CHAPTER FIVE

At the end of the next week the results for the high
school sculpture competition were announced.
They were announced in Stephanie's art class and
then broadcast to the entire school in the late afternoon. Out of two dozen entries the sculpture that
had been chosen over all others was Stephanie's.
She almost couldn't believe it. When Mr. Hassam
told her who the winner was she asked if he was
sure – if he was really sure. She'd never considered
actually winning the competition, or even thought
about it – much. She'd never taken winning as a real
possibility. For the rest of the afternoon she sat
through classes in a kind of stupor while various
people crowded up to her and congratulated her
on winning. It all seemed completely unreal, something seen through a haze: out of focus and shim-
mering.

When she got home the news had sunk in a little
further. Then the anxiety of completing the project
overwhelmed her. Stephanie burst into the empty
house, shed her coat and boots by the door,

dropped her books on the floor and raced to the kitchen phone. Her cold fingers fumbled over the numbers. Two rings. Three rings. Someone picked it up.

"Mum."

"Hi Steph."

"Mum, I won."

"Won what?"

"The sculpture competition. At school."

"That's wonderful!"

"No it's not."

"It's not?"

"No," wailed Stephanie. "Because now that I've won it I actually have to build it."

"So?"

"So. You don't know about the dimensions I put down."

"Dimensions?"

"For the sculpture. They're incredibly large. I just can't do it." Stephanie collapsed against the door-frame. "Large," she moaned into the phone. "Large. Big. Huge. Terrible."

"You're such a dramatic child."

"But it's so big. I mean if I'd known I was going to win I would have made it smaller."

"Didn't you think you might win?"

32

"No."

"Then why did you enter?"

"Well. Maybe I did think about it. Maybe once. But only a little. Not enough to think it might really happen."

"You're too hasty." Her mother sounded irritated. "You don't spend enough time thinking things through."

"I'm not. And I do," said Stephanie, who knew she was and she didn't.

"Hold on a minute Steph." Her mother's voice got faint and she seemed to be talking to someone else. Stephanie waited, slumped against the doorframe, for her mother to get back on the line.

"Steph?"

"Hi."

"Sorry."

"Are you busy?"

"Really busy."

"Do you want me to hang up?"

"No. No I don't."

"Good." Stephanie hated it when she had to suddenly break off conversations with her mother because she was too busy at work.

"It sounds like you need help with your sculpture. If it's that large you can't do it all by yourself."

"I'll be lucky if I can do any of it myself."

"Why don't you organize a group of your friends to help for the final stages? For the casting and the erecting."

Stephanie thought for a moment. It was true that she would need more help for the actual physical work of the project, not so much for the planning and diagram stage.

"I could do that. If I could find anybody who'd want to work on it."

"I bet you wouldn't have any problem. Just ask."

Stephanie thought again.

"Alright," she said after a while. "I will." She twisted the telephone cord with her free hand. "But what about the bones?"

"What about the bones?"

"Well, I mean they're dinosaur bones."

"So?"

"So I don't know anything about making dinosaur bones. I don't know what kind of bones or how big to make them, or anything."

"Couldn't you have considered this before you began the project?" Her mother sounded irritated again.

"No."

"But you know a lot about bones. It's your

34

hobby."

"It's not my hobby," said Stephanie fiercely. "It's bigger than a hobby. It's what I'm going to be."

"Sorry."

"I do know about bones. Dinosaur bones. I just don't know *exactly*. And I have to know *exactly* to be able to do this. I don't want to do it wrong. You don't understand."

"No, I do. I do."

There was a silence. Stephanie's mother said something to someone in her office.

"Steph, there's a woman I know here. One of the authors of the social science text book series I've been working on. She's a paleontologist. A retired paleontology professor actually. She retired last year I think. Anyway, maybe she'd be able to help you with the dinosaur information."

"Do you think so?"

"We can try. Look, I'll give her a call. And then I'll call you back. Ok?"

"Ok."

They hung up.

Stephanie sat down on a chair, waiting for the phone to ring. She picked up an apple from the wooden bowl and rolled it back and forth across the table between her palms. Maybe having the sculpture so large wouldn't be as bad as she thought. It would certainly be prominent. It might even be spectacular. And it would be there forever, until time and weather wore it down. When she was an old woman she could walk past it and remember how it was when she'd won, when she'd built it. The thought of her older future self being proud of her young present self pleased Stephanie. She rubbed the apple on her sweater and began to eat it.

The phone rang.

"Hi Mum."

"Hi Steph."

"Did you get her?"

"Yes. It's fine with her. Delighted is what I think she said. I'll give you the address when I get home. I said you'd go over there tomorrow after school, ok?"

"Ok."

"Her name's Kate Burton."

"Ok."

"And Steph, do you think you could make a salad? There's stuff in the fridge. I might be a little late tonight, don't wait if you don't want to."

Stephanie took a bite of the apple.

"I'll wait."

CHAPTER SIX

While Stephanie walked to school the next morning she made up a list of everything she was worried about. She did this periodically as a way of keeping track of her problems and of putting them in the correct priority. This morning her list was extremely short.

1) Anne Delaney
2) Dinosaur sculpture

They were both, of course, very big, weighty problems and Stephanie felt she could only do something constructive about one of them. She concentrated on the dinosaur sculpture. Maybe this Burton woman would have some suggestions about building the bones. What she had to do before she went and saw Kate Burton was to organize a work party for the project. She'd have to ask people at school if they wanted to help in the final construction. Maybe she'd make an announcement in art class.

Stephanie walked to school along a series of roads, through a field and through a plaza parking lot. It was barely a fifteen minute walk but she seemed to do her best thinking en route to school. It was while walking to school that she'd first decided she liked Anne Delaney. It was also while walking to school that she decided to pursue her interest in bones and become a paleontologist. But it annoyed Stephanie that she suddenly came upon a realization, as if from nowhere. She had a feeling that beneath her sudden understanding there was another kind of thinking, but she couldn't really follow it. Everything seemed to happen all of a sudden and was always a surprise. Stephanie was getting a little sick of constantly being alarmed by her thoughts. Couldn't she start having nice, safe predictable ones? Maybe she could try. Maybe she could just think about nice, safe, predictable things and then she would have nice, safe, predictable thoughts.

For the remainder of the journey to school Stephanie concentrated on thinking about laundry and dishes. But laundry made her think of clothes and clothes of sweaters and sweaters made her think, very intensely, of Anne Delaney. Dishes were not much better either. Dishes led to porcelain. Porcelain to bone china. Bone china to bones. Bones of dinosaurs and the dinosaur project. So there it was.

No matter what she started out thinking about it always ended up that she was thinking about her two great preoccupations: 1) Anne Delaney 2) Dinosaur sculpture. Stephanie wondered if it would be possible to try and give up thinking altogether.

Before the beginning of art class Stephanie asked Mr. Hassam if she could make an announcement at the end of the period.

"About the sculpture?" he asked.

"About the sculpture," said Stephanie gloomily.

All through class she tried to word the announcement. She tried to think of a good opening sentence. "I was wondering if …" "As you probably already know I've won this – contest – thing …" "Please. I need help." But each one she thought of sounded more ridiculous than the one before and when it came time for her to actually make the announcement, and Mr. Hassam called her from her seat to the front of the class, she felt totally confused and had no idea of what to say.

Silence.

Someone in the back row coughed.

Stephanie stared at her shoelaces. They were getting frayed.

More silence.

"Well," she said and then stopped.

"I've won this sculpture thing," she tried again. "And I can't do all the building myself. I mean, the dimensions. It's huge."

Silence.

"I need help for the final part. For casting it and putting it all together. It wouldn't take all that long," she put in hastily. "And it might be kind of fun," she continued, trying to be positive for her audience of classmates.

Luckily at this point, before she had to think up something else to say, Mr. Hassam cut in and suggested that perhaps the work on the sculpture could be credited towards his art class. People began to volunteer. In five minutes Stephanie had the promised assistance of ten people and began to feel much better about the whole thing. Among those who lent their support to the project were Devi and Eric Sullivan.

Later in the day, at the end of history class, something happened that terrified and elated Stephanie. As she was bending over her desk, packing up her books and thinking about the sculpture work party she heard her name being called. Looking up slowly, still thinking about dinosaurs, she found herself staring at the face of Anne Delaney. She wanted to die.

"Eric told me you needed help building your sculpture." There it was. Anne Delaney had spoken to her, to Stephanie. Stephanie suddenly felt that she didn't know who she was anymore. She tried to find her voice and managed to drag it out from somewhere deep inside herself.

"Do I?" No. No. Wrong way around. Stupid. Stupid. The other way.

"I mean, I do."

"Well I'd like to help. I don't know what I could do, but it sounds pretty good." Anne Delaney spoke so effortlessly, standing there with her books tucked loosely under her arm.

"Will you let me know when you need me?"

This was almost too much for Stephanie to bear. She looked down at the floor.

"Sure," she said, her voice coming out deep and mumbly because of the angle of her head.

"What?"

Stephanie lifted her head and looked Anne Delaney right in the eyes. Green eyes. Green eyes with little gold flecks in them.

"Sure. I'll let you know. That would be great."

Stephanie watched Anne Delaney walk out of the history room. She almost didn't believe it had happened. Dialogue. And Anne Delaney hadn't seemed to notice how nervous Stephanie had been. Stephanie scooped her books off her desk. But how would she get any work done on the sculpture if Anne was there? She'd be constantly distracted. What would happen when her two problems were together in the same place?

"Stephanie." She turned to see Eric Sullivan jogging down the hall towards her.

"Hi." He stopped and didn't seem like he had anything to say, even though he'd called out to her so urgently.

"I think your sculpture's going to be really great," he said, staring at the floor. "I'm going to like working on it."

"It's great that you want to help," said Stephanie, shifting her books from one arm to the other. "I can use all the help I can get."

"I was wondering," began Eric, still intently watching the space of tile in front of his left toe. "If – if – you'd like to go out with me sometime. Maybe to a movie? Maybe this Friday?"

"Oh no," thought Stephanie. She looked at Eric's bent head and wondered what to say. She didn't want to go out with him. She didn't really like him. But he looked so nervous she felt sorry for him. And everyone else went out with boys.

"I'm kind of busy right now with the dinosaur thing," she said.

"Oh."

Silence.

Stephanie felt even more sorry for him.

"But maybe another time," she said before she could stop herself.

Eric looked a lot happier.

"Ok," he said and started off towards his next class. "Soon," he called over his shoulder and Stephanie echoed the word back to him. "Soon."

Maybe soon would never come. Maybe Eric would start liking someone else and forget all about asking her out again. Maybe she could just avoid him for the rest of high school.

Stephanie walked quickly down the hall, hoping that nothing else would happen to her that day. It all seemed to be too much.

CHAPTER SEVEN

Kate Burton lived outside of the city in an old brick house with a big wooden front porch and a door on the outside of the second storey that led to nowhere. Stephanie had to take two buses and then walk through the snow for fifteen minutes to get there. By the time she arrived she was feeling tired from the happenings at school that day and from travelling. She almost didn't feel up to meeting a stranger and having to dwell, yet again, on the problems of the dinosaur project.

The door was answered after the third knock by a short thin woman with grey hair and glasses. She reminded Stephanie of her grandmother, who had lived with them once, a long, long, time ago, but who had died five years previously.

"Hi," she said, a little hesitantly. "I'm Stephanie Powell."

"Hello Stephanie Powell." The eyes behind the glasses were bright and lively. "Come in." The door was held open. "It must be freezing out there in the world."

"It is freezing," said Stephanie fiercely. "I'm freezing."

Kate Burton laughed. "You sound mad."

"I am mad," said Stephanie. "No I'm not really mad. I'm annoyed. I get annoyed all the time these days. Sometimes for no reason."

"It goes with the age."

"Does it?" Stephanie stepped into the warm hallway.

"I remember," said Kate Burton, pushing the door gently shut, "being your age and hating everything – thinking that everything and everyone was there primarily to make my life hell."

"It goes away – doesn't it?" Stephanie followed her into a large living room filled with bookcases. There was a fire in the fireplace.

"Of course it goes away. Let me take your coat and then you can warm up by the fire."

Stephanie dutifully handed over her coat and went and stood beside the cradle of flame.

"There are many good aspects to your age. You should concentrate on them." The voice was muffled and it seemed to Stephanie as if Kate Burton was speaking from deep inside a closet. She spread her hands out over the flames and felt the first prickling of heat at her fingers. She liked this

46

house. It felt friendly and comfortable. She wished that she hadn't said that stuff about being constantly annoyed. It was definitely the wrong sort of thing to say to someone you'd just met. But it had just slipped out and Stephanie was finding that it was harder and harder to keep anything in. Everything in her, all her thoughts and feelings, seemed desperate to get out into words, and most of the time she couldn't do anything to stop it. It didn't appear to be something she had any reasonable control over.

Kate Burton had come back into the living room.

"We cut down a tree," she said. "Maple. Massive thing. So we should have enough wood for the entire winter."

"Why do you have a door at the top of your house that goes nowhere?" asked Stephanie, turning from the fire.

"I think there must have been a balcony there once. Or else it was a way to dispose of unwanted guests." She smiled. "We keep it locked now."

Stephanie wondered if she was an unwanted guest. After all she had kind of forced this woman's help by using her mother's influence.

"Would you like some dinner?"

"Dinner." Stephanie realized suddenly that it was

quite late and that she hadn't had anything to eat since her lunch at noon. A sandwich and an apple.

"Yes, dinner. That meal that is often consumed in the latter part of the day."

"Sure. Yes. That'd be great."

"And after dinner we can discuss your project."

"Oh, my project." Stephanie felt the cloud of doom descend. Up until it was mentioned she'd completely forgotten about her reason for being there.

"You sound depressed about it."

"Not depressed exactly." Stephanie struggled to find the correct words. "Kind of scared and anxious."

"Well that's natural. It's a perfectly healthy reaction to get nervous about something you care about."

"It is?"

"It is."

Stephanie followed Kate Burton out of the living room and down the hall to the kitchen, a large room with a big wooden trestle table in the middle and walls that were covered in what looked to be old newspaper articles.

"I made a stew," said Kate, going over to the stove. "Because I didn't know if you'd want to eat or not and this way there's plenty for whatever you decided."

"Stew. Sounds great." Stephanie tried to forget that she'd been subjected to stew for much of the past week.

There was a sound at the door from the kitchen to the backyard and Stephanie turned in the direction of the noise. A woman, taller and younger than Kate Burton pushed through the entrance. Her clothes were covered in snow and she stamped heavily on the mat by the door.

"There you are," said Kate, not turning around from the stove. "I thought I'd have to come and get you."

"I had a few contemplative moments on the way back from the sheep." The woman was still shaking snow from her clothes.

Kate Burton turned to face them both. "Mary," she said to the woman. "This is Stephanie Powell."

"Anne's daughter?"

"Yes, Anne's daughter."

"Ah," said the woman named Mary. "You're the one who's doing that thing with bones."

"Sculpture," put in Kate Burton.

"No," said Stephanie, "right now it's more of a thing than a sculpture."

49

"Sit down," said Kate, "and I'll serve." Both Mary and Stephanie sat obediently down.

"You have sheep?" asked Stephanie.

"A few," said Mary.

"Four," said Kate.

"Four," repeated Mary. "We don't have them for any particular reason. We just have them."

"We have them for aggravation," said Kate, bringing over bowls of stew.

"We have each other for that. We just have the sheep because we do." Mary shrugged and reached for the salt. "Tell me about your thing with bones."

Stephanie had again momentarily forgotten about her thing with bones.

"Could I use your bathroom?" she asked, deciding it would be less impolite to go before the meal rather than during it. Also it would enable her to avoid answering Mary's question.

"Top of the stairs and to the right." Kate pointed out in the direction of the hall.

At the top of the stairs and to the left were two rooms. The doors were open. Stephanie decided to just have a peek inside before she went to the bathroom. The first room was obviously a study, lined with books and with a big desk monopolizing almost an entire wall. The second room was a bedroom. Closets. Clothes thrown over a chair by the window. A double bed in the centre of the room. Stephanie backed discreetly out of the doorway and looked down the hall past the bathroom. There was another room at the end of the hall. She tiptoed quietly towards it. This room was a studio. There was a drafting table and brushes and lots of things with paint on them. Stephanie heard the companionable lilt of voices downstairs and felt guilty for having snuck around. She headed back to the bathroom, shut the door and stood in front of the mirror looking at herself. If there was only one bedroom and only one bed then it must mean that Kate Burton and Mary whatever-her-last-name-was must sleep in it – *together*. She found that she wasn't that surprised, as if she'd known this from Kate Burton's first mention of "we." She found it a little exciting, and for one brief, splendid moment she had a vision of herself and Anne Delaney living in one room and sleeping in one bed.

"Stephanie," yelled a voice from beneath her, startling her into feeling guilty again. "Are you lost?"

"No. I'll be right down."

CHAPTER EIGHT

The day before Mark was to leave to take up residence in university the family had dinner together. Over the past few years Stephanie couldn't remember the last time they'd all eaten together, aside from the usual obligatory family dinners at birthdays and Christmas. Mark was often not there at mealtimes, staying late at school or out with friends. Stephanie ate soon after getting home from school, or sometimes waited for her mother to return home from work. Her father often worked the late shift at the printing plant and arrived back around midnight. He usually ate by himself in the kitchen, with that one light on in an otherwise dark house.

It was almost awkward when they sat down together for dinner, on Mark's last night at home. There was silence for a while and then small talk about the meal. Following that there was small talk about Mark and school and his plans for the year. It wasn't until dessert that Stephanie could get around to mentioning what she wanted. Now that she'd found out about the one bedroom at Kate Burton's house she was dying to know if her parents were aware of this. And if they were, what did they think? Talking about Kate Burton seemed a good way to test them about homosexuality. It was a hard thing to bring up though. There didn't seem to be a place in the conversation where she could slip it in.

"You know Ms. Burton?" she finally managed to ask her mother.

"Oh, how did that go Stephanie?" interjected Mr. Powell.

"It went fine."

"Was she any help?"

"She was great. We chose the bones and decided how many. And we did some drawings – sketches. I'm going over there tomorrow afternoon to work on it some more."

"What about Kate?" asked her mother.

"Kate Burton?" Mark looked up from his plate. "Didn't I meet her at your Christmas party last year?"

"Yes, I think she was there."

Stephanie was getting nowhere. Maybe she shouldn't bother. She was pretty sure about her father's reaction to the topic of homosexuality. But her mother? What did her mother think? Did her mother know about Kate Burton? Her curiosity got the better of her.

"There's this woman named Mary who lives in her house."

"Mary Gunther," offered her mother.

"Was she at the Christmas party last year? I don't remember her?"

"Mark," said Stephanie in exasperation. "How can you remember anything about the Christmas party? You drank too much and were sick and had to go to bed at about ten o'clock."

"Did I?"

"Mum," said Stephanie. "How long has that Mary …"

"Mary Gunther."

"Mary Gunther. How long has she been living with Ms. Burton?"

Mrs. Powell cut herself a small second piece of pie.

"About twenty-five years I think."

"Twenty-five years!" Stephanie couldn't imagine living with anyone for that length of time. It always amazed her that her parents weren't sick to death of each other after twenty years; although sometimes it seemed that they were.

"Are they sisters or something?" asked Mark, who finally seemed to have caught up to the conversation.

"No." Mrs. Powell looked quite serious.

Stephanie shot a glance at her brother, almost certain of what he would say next.

"Well, Mum," he said. "There must be something going on between them. People don't live together for no reason."

"Mark," his mother looked at him sternly. "You shouldn't just assume things."

"Mum," said Stephanie. "When I was there I saw that they only have one bedroom. And," she paused dramatically, "they only have one bed."

There, it had been said. She felt light-headed with nervousness. She felt that perhaps she shouldn't have said anything. What if they connected this fascination with Kate Burton's bedroom to her and her feelings for Anne Delaney? No, they couldn't know. Could they? Stephanie thought she might be losing her mind.

Mrs. Powell looked at both her children.

"What Kate Burton and Mary Gunther do is their own business and no one else's."

Stephanie felt relief rush over her. She had known. And she didn't seem to mind. Stephanie loved her mother.

Mr. Powell, who, up until this moment had been silent, now decided it was time for his opinion to be heard.

"It's not normal Anne. I think it's perfectly natural that the children would be concerned."

"We're not concerned," said Mark quickly. "We're curious."

"Maybe," continued her father. "Stephanie shouldn't go back to that house again. It's not a good influence for a young girl to have."

Stephanie felt like screaming out – "I have to go back there again," because she felt that it was imperative she return. Why did her father want to wreck her life? Why was he sometimes so unfair?

"Don't be so ridiculous," her mother snapped at her father. "Being different shouldn't be likened to being guilty. It isn't a crime."

"It is in some parts of the world."

They were arguing now and when they argued they usually argued for hours. Mark and Stephanie rose simultaneously, left the dinner table and went upstairs. They stood in the hall between their two bedrooms, not really wanting to go into their separate rooms. Even though they were older it still made them uneasy when their parents fought. It made them feel as if they were still little kids.

"Why do you think Dad's so bad about some things?" asked Stephanie.

"I don't know," Mark shrugged. "He's always hated lots of stuff. I guess that's just the way it is with him."

Stephanie sighed. "I think he hates more than he likes. Was he always like that?"

"I can't remember." Mark frowned. "I can only think of him the way he is now. I can't remember him younger. I can only remember us younger."

"Me too." Stephanie turned away from the voices in the kitchen.

"What time are you leaving in the morning?"

"Early. John's coming over to help with the last of my stuff."

"I don't think I want to get up and stand around in the driveway freezing to watch you leave."

There was an awkward silence. "Well," said Mark finally. "You'll probably see more of me now because when I come home to visit I'll actually be here and won't always be out the way I am now."

"And I can visit you," said Stephanie. "You're not exactly far away."

But it didn't matter that what they said to one another was true. It didn't matter that they were going to see each other twice next week. It felt like something was over. It felt like goodbye. And for Stephanie it didn't matter what something was but rather what it felt like. Emotions always overpowered reason and fact.

Stephanie gave her brother a quick hug and with mumbled goodnights they retreated into their respective bedrooms.

Stephanie lay on her bed with her hands behind her head and stared at the ceiling. She thought about her brother leaving and how alone it made her feel. There was no longer another representative of her generation to stand up to the opinions and decrees of her parents. She would have to face them alone from now on. It would be a lot harder without Mark there on her side.

She thought about Kate Burton and Mary Gunther and about how there was only one bed and what her parents had said (and were still saying) about that. She thought about Anne Delaney offering to help on the dinosaur project and about how it would be impossible to concentrate on the dinosaur if Anne Delaney was there too.

She thought about the dinosaur and what needed to be done before the sculpture would be ready to be erected for the spring. There were so many details to pay attention to; so many things to watch out for. She thought about lists and made one up for the things she was thinking of, in alphabetical order. She thought about growing older. She thought about what it would be like to live with the same person for twenty-five years. She thought she should do some of the dinosaur sketches. She fell asleep.

CHAPTER NINE

In school the next week Stephanie put concentration and thought into her schoolwork, which had lately been suffering from her other, more immediate, concerns. She paid attention in class (even in History and English) and managed to get all her homework done as well as spend time on the dinosaur sculpture. Towards the end of the week she was feeling good about everything again.

On Thursday Eric Sullivan asked her out and this time she said yes. She hadn't thought about him since the last time he'd asked her out. Eric didn't often come into her thoughts. But he'd looked so shy and awkward and – well – sincere on Thursday that she said yes before she could stop herself. She felt sorry for him. Stephanie knew what it was to like someone and not know if they liked you back, or if they even paid attention to your existence. So, realizing it was probably for all the wrong reasons Stephanie had agreed to go out to a movie the following evening with Eric Sullivan.

Her parents were a bit too enthusiastic about the

news and Stephanie had to keep telling them that she didn't really like Eric and that it wasn't such a big deal. But they persisted in their enthusiasm and Stephanie finally just gave up. They didn't seem to understand her at all anymore and she certainly couldn't understand why they'd be so excited about a stupid date to see a movie. Maybe they were just being excited for her because they thought it was what she wanted. What would they do if they really knew what she wanted? What would they do if she went on a date with Anne Delaney?

In a very strange way Stephanie got her wish and did go on a date with Anne Delaney. For when Friday evening appeared and Eric came to pick her up in his parents' car he informed her that it was a double date, with his friend Steve and Steve's date – Anne Delaney.

All the way to the movie Stephanie was silent while Anne and Steve and Eric talked back and forth between the seats. She felt too panic-stricken to even open her mouth. It seemed like some kind of terrible practical joke. Just when she felt in control of her life again and somewhat alright up popped Anne Delaney, to completely throw her off balance. On the drive to the movie, past the plazas and gas stations and small snow-covered lawns, she actually felt herself hating Anne Delaney. She had no right to make Stephanie endure such hell. She was cruel. And inhuman. And too beautiful. And too smart. And how could she laugh at Steve's jokes which weren't even funny? How could she be so friendly and casual? How well did she know Steve anyway? Did they go out? They sounded too comfortable together for this to be their first date.

In the line for tickets Anne Delaney again expressed her interest in Stephanie's sculpture.

"How's the dinosaur going?" she asked.

"Fine." Stephanie felt incapable of saying any more. She stared intently at a movie poster on the opposite wall.

"When are you going to be ready to put it up?"

"Soon."

At this second futile attempt at conversation Anne Delaney gave up and went back to talking to Steve. Stephanie was almost grateful.

In the movie theatre she found to her horror that the way they had entered the row of seats meant that she had to sit beside Anne Delaney. Eric sat on Stephanie's right, Steve on Anne's left. Stephanie squished herself over in her seat to avoid getting close to Anne and concentrated on talking to Eric, who, up until this point she had virtually ignored.

They talked about History class and the upcoming test. They talked about the dinosaur – briefly, and about Eric's part-time job in the grocery store for longer. And all the while she talked, when she said yes and no and asked what she hoped were interesting questions, Stephanie felt the presence of Anne Delaney grow stronger and stronger beside her. And she felt more and more scared and anxious and strangely excited. When the lights dimmed to signal the start of the movie she could have cried with relief. Now at least she had an excuse to be silent and nothing was required of her but to watch the screen.

For the first half of the movie everything was alright. Stephanie followed the story with no difficulty and managed to concentrate only on what was happening in the film, shutting out everything that was happening in her head. But after the first hour she was lost. The woman who sat in front of Anne Delaney had tall hair and so Anne shifted in her seat to be able to see the movie. She shifted in the direction of Stephanie and her moving caused their arms to touch on the armrest. Anne's head was dangerously close to Stephanie's left shoulder. Stephanie could even hear Anne's breathing next to her ear. It was no use. She couldn't pay any attention at all to the images flickering on the movie screen. She felt almost ill. Her mind was screaming something unintelligible and her heart was convulsing in her chest. For a moment she honestly thought she might die.

If Stephanie had had any doubts before about her feelings for Anne Delaney they all disappeared the instant Anne's arm had come in contact with her own. Now she had no doubts at all about what she felt. She "liked" Anne Delaney, whatever that meant, whatever limits that stretched to. But she also wanted to touch Anne Delaney. It was as if her body had suddenly come to life after a very long sleep. All her nerves were standing at attention, ready for orders. She wanted to touch Anne Delaney. She wanted Anne Delaney to touch her. She wanted to lean over, through the darkness of the theatre, and kiss her.

Stephanie wanted to do none of these things with Eric Sullivan. Although she liked him well enough and could talk to him fairly easily she didn't feel her body drawn to his the way her body was drawn to Anne's. The entire physical aspect was absent in her feelings for Eric. It was as if he was her brother, or a friend.

She sat through the movie with her arm warm

where it touched Anne's arm, praying that Anne would move, praying that she wouldn't. And she felt almost happy. Anne never did move her arm away, not until the credits swallowed up the screen and the lights in the theatre went on.

On the drive back home the others talked about the movie while Stephanie stared out the window. She could still feel the pressure on her arm where Anne had touched it and she was concentrating on remembering how it felt. She wanted to be able to remember how it felt for her entire lifetime, which, at the moment seemed entirely possible.

Steve and Anne were dropped off first and then Eric drove Stephanie home. She gave him a quick kiss at the front door, told him how much fun it had been and escaped quickly into the safety of her house.

Once inside she leaned against the front door, feeling relieved that the evening was over.

CHAPTER TEN

Stephanie spent the next few weeks trying not to think of Anne Delaney and to concentrate only on school and the dinosaur sculpture. This was only partially successful as it seemed that no matter what she thought about everything was, or became, Anne Delaney.

It was a Saturday afternoon and Stephanie was spending the day at Kate and Mary's house. She and Kate had progressed from sketching the dinosaur bones that would be used to constructing a miniature clay model of the actual sculpture. This miniature, called a maquette, would be the working model for the final sculpture so it was important that the dimensions (even though they were scaled down) be completely accurate. They were working on the maquette up in Mary's studio because the light was good for such detailed work and because Mary wouldn't mind if they got blobs of clay stuck on various surfaces of the room. Mary seemed to possess endless good nature.

"You know," said Kate, squinting at one of their

many diagrams and surveying the lump of clay in front of her on the table. "This is hard."

Stephanie had already reached this conclusion long ago.

"I think," she said, "that if I had to do this every day I'd go crazy."

Kate rolled up her sleeves and poked at the clay.

"It might take us most of the weekend."

"Forever," intoned Stephanie, who was becoming quite accustomed to the concept of forever.

"Do you mind?" she asked, suddenly feeling a little guilty for all the work Kate had done.

"Forever?"

"No, the weekend."

"This is the most fun I've had in ages. The most fun," Kate looked at the diagrams again, "since Mary and I pruned trees last summer and I got stuck."

"You got stuck up a tree?"

"Well Mary's afraid of heights so it was me who had to climb the trees and cut the branches. She held the ladder."

Stephanie pictured Kate Burton climbing trees and almost laughed.

"And I couldn't get down from this one tree." Kate started shaping a miniature dinosaur leg bone from one of the bits of clay. "I mean it was quite impossible for me to move at all. I just couldn't do it. I was stuck."

"So this is as much fun as getting stuck in a tree?" Somehow Stephanie couldn't see the connection being a flattering one.

"Because it's unexpected. Because it's outside of my usual experience. That's what makes it so enjoyable."

"I don't know if I'd call it enjoyable."

"What would you call it then?"

"Terminal." Stephanie grinned. "Terminal project. Terminal dinosaur."

Kate Burton tilted her head back and laughed. The sun sliding through the windows made the white in her hair sparkle and for that moment Stephanie thought she looked like a young woman.

"What were you like when you were my age?" she asked.

"Like I am now I suppose. A little more impatient and eager. But I don't think people change a great deal when they age. They just seem to become more themselves."

"Do you like being old?"

"Am I old?"

Stephanie felt embarrassed.

"You're older than me," she said hesitantly. "That's probably what I meant."

"Yes. I do. I feel better about myself, and calmer. I think it's important to like who you are. At any age."

"I'm not sure if I know who I am."

Kate looked over at Stephanie.

"But aren't you beginning to find out?"

Stephanie wasn't sure she wanted to find out any more than she already knew. What if there was more? She could barely handle what was there already. To have more to deal with would be simply unbearable.

They worked in silence for a while, applying their attention to the maquette. Once they'd started making the bones it wasn't nearly as hard as it had appeared. Everything had been carefully marked out on the diagrams and they just followed these "maps." They were able to make a lot of progress. Stephanie liked the way they worked together. The fact that there could be silence as well as conversation and that it was all very easy and relaxed. She had begun to think of Kate Burton not as merely a friend of her mother's, but also as a friend of her own.

"What do you think the most important thing in

life is?" she asked after a while.

Kate considered this for several minutes.

"Being happy," she said finally. "No," she changed her mind. "Not being happy."

"Being unhappy?"

"No, no. I meant it's not being happy ... never mind what I meant."

"What do you think it is then?"

Kate considered again.

"Satisfaction," she said. "Being satisfied with yourself and your world. And if you're not satisfied, feeling confident enough to make changes so that you will be."

Stephanie thought about this for a while. It made a lot of sense. She wondered if she'd ever feel satisfied. With anything.

"Do you think I'll ever be satisfied?"

"Of course. If you make efforts in your life to improve."

"You think I need improving?"

"I think you're young."

"I am young." Stephanie was beginning to feel a little annoyed at the direction the conversation was taking. "I can't help it if I'm young. It's not my fault." She almost said, "I didn't ask to be born," but managed to stop herself.

Kate Burton appeared to be smiling at a dinosaur rib.

"I didn't mean it as an insult."

Stephanie didn't want to talk about being satisfied anymore. It only reminded her that she wasn't and made her feel depressed. What she wanted to do was to talk about Anne Delaney. About her feelings for Anne and about what it might or did mean. She wanted to ask Kate Burton about her relationship with Mary. About if she had the same feeling for Mary as Stephanie had for Anne. She wanted to ask if it felt wrong. Because, to Stephanie, though she knew that being so different from other people wasn't wrong, it still felt that way sometimes. And she wanted to say that word, that word that made it all sound so – well – definite. She wanted to ask: "Kate, do you think I could be a lesbian? Do you think I'd know yet?"

She said nothing.

She couldn't.

When she opened her mouth to ask these questions there was no voice for them to arrive through. There was not even a sound. Nothing.

They worked on the maquette for the rest of the afternoon and by five o'clock they'd finished. It looked quite professional and actually had the correct dimensions. It actually looked like a dinosaur head, although it lost some of its intended impact being so small. They went and had tea together in the kitchen with the long wooden table and the newspaper on the walls. They talked about the dinosaur. About how, when the bones were cast they would have to be placed carefully together or else it wouldn't look like a head. It would look like a heap of mismatched bones. It wouldn't look as if they were mismatched on purpose.

CHAPTER ELEVEN

Stephanie was in the public library. She was sitting at a table near the back with books scattered over the surface in front of her. She was doing some final research for the dinosaur project – checking and double-checking the dimensions of the bones. The actual construction of the bones was due to begin the following week and she wanted to make sure there hadn't been any mistakes made on the calculations. It had gone so smoothly so far that she was suspicious. She thought there must be something they'd overlooked, but she hadn't found anything wrong yet.

Stephanie had been in the library for at least three hours. Only the last hour had been spent looking at dinosaur bone books. Her justification for coming to the library had been to check the bone statistics. Her real reason for coming to the library had been to read about homosexuality. For two hours she had dragged every relevant book she could find from the shelves. She'd taken them back to her table and carefully hidden them inside the dinosaur books. Just in case someone was looking. A lot of the titles were in LARGE CAPITAL LETTERS and she was sure they could be seen across the entire library.

She had methodically combed each one for references to her particular situation. There were, however, no references to her particular situation; maybe, she reasoned, after discovering this, because no one else was in her exact situation. Everybody's life was different.

She did find out certain facts from reading through the books. She found out that one in ten people was gay. She found out that no one really knew why people were gay, whether it was a learned behaviour or was genetic.

Stephanie liked facts. She liked the finality of them. She liked statistics and charts and lists. Reading about homosexuality made Stephanie feel less isolated in her feelings. But not all that she read made her feel good. The health texts, the books with the facts, were fine because a fact was a nice neutral thing. It didn't say "bad" or "good" or "right" or "wrong." It said "this is this." Like naming the different types of cloud formations. It just told you how many there were and what they were. But there were also books with testimonials from gay people and from the families of these people. These were more unsettling. Fact wasn't important there. Emotion was. And often the emotions weren't very appealing. Stephanie read about one woman who told her family she was a lesbian and because of that they would have nothing more to do with her. They disowned her. Another woman had told her parents but they refused to believe it was true. They seemed incapable of believing it. They still asked her if she'd met any nice men lately. They expected her to grow out of it, as though it were some adolescent phase. The woman was in her forties.

Stephanie closed the last dinosaur book and piled it on top of the others by her left elbow. She wished she could talk to someone about all this. About her feelings. About Anne Delaney. About the possibility of her being a lesbian. But who could she tell? Her parents? Stephanie imagined how a discussion with her parents might go:

Stephanie: I think I'm in love with Anne Delaney.

Her Father: What a strange name for a boy. Who would call their son Anne?

Stephanie: It's not a boy. It's not an it either. She's a girl. Anne Delaney.

Her Mother: Oh dear.

Her Father: A girl?

Stephanie: Well I don't really understand it either. It just kind of happened.

Her Mother: I thought we did all the right things with you. What did we do wrong?

Her Father: It's a sickness. It has nothing to do with us. It's a perversion.

Her Mother: It's not a perversion. Or a sickness. But I didn't think – well – not in our family.

Stephanie stopped. She was getting depressed by the imagined confrontation. No, she couldn't talk to her parents. Mark? They'd always told each other everything, since they'd been old enough to talk. He was her friend and confidant and had known her forever. And he didn't have a problem with people's differences. He was ok. But she'd already tried to say something before to him and it hadn't worked. She didn't know what to say or how to start saying it.

Stephanie wondered if she'd ever have enough courage to say anything to Anne Delaney. But what could she say?

Stephanie: I think I'm in love with you.

Anne: In love? With me?

Stephanie: With you.

Anne: With me?

Stephanie: Yes, with you.

Anne: Why?

No. It was impossible. She already knew that Anne didn't like her. She felt it somewhere inside herself. Anne liked Steve. Anne liked boys. The only reason she was at all interested in Stephanie was because of the dinosaur. Anne Delaney liked the dinosaur.

Stephanie: You're in love with my dinosaur.

Anne: I know. I can't help myself.

Stephanie: But it's dead. It's past dead. It's extinct. It's a non-existence. It's....

Anne: It's wonderful.

Stephanie: But why can't you love me. I'm not extinct.

Anne: Is that the only recommendation you can offer?

No. It was best to concentrate on her feelings for Anne Delaney. Figure out what they were and what they meant and try and forget about Anne Delaney herself. Maybe, in one weird way Anne Delaney wasn't as important as the feelings Stephanie had about her.

Stephanie: You're not as important as the way I feel about you.

Anne: What?

Stephanie: You're less important....

Anne: Thanks a lot!

Stephanie sighed. Why couldn't things work out the way you wanted them to? People were always saying that things worked out for the best but maybe they only said that so they'd feel better about the way things did work out. So it was easier to put up with what they didn't want.

Stephanie sighed again. Why were there always better questions than answers?

"Hi."

She looked up quickly to see Devi standing beside her with an armload of books.

"Devi. What are you doing here?" She put an arm protectively over the books on the table.

Devi looked at her strangely.

"I come to the library a lot. I have a card." She shifted the books from one arm to the other. "I take out stuff for my grandmother, in Hindi. She can't get outside much in the winter."

"Oh."

"What are you doing here?"

Stephanie realized she was gripping the edge of her pile of books so hard that her hand was beginning to ache.

"Dinosaurs. Dimensions."

"Are you alright?" Devi put her books down on the table and leaned over Stephanie. "You look a little funny."

"I'm fine."

"Let's see."

"What?"

"One of the books. I like all those pictures of dinosaurs. I like their teeth."

Devi reached under Stephanie's arm and pried out the top book on the stack. Stephanie felt like dying. Underneath the dinosaur book was one of the homosexuality books. The one with a title in LARGE CAPITAL LETTERS. She threw both arms over the book. But Devi had seen it.

"What's that?"

"What?"

"That." Devi tapped a portion of the title not covered by Stephanie's arms.

"Someone left them here," lied Stephanie. "I was going to take them over to the return table with my books. My dinosaur books."

Devi was silent for a moment.

"Move your arms," she said.

Stephanie moved her arms.

"I thought so." Devi put the unopened dinosaur book on the table.

"You thought what?" asked Stephanie, wildly trying to stall what seemed inevitable.

"I thought I recognized it. My parents have that book."

It was the book with the testimonials.

"I've seen it on the bookcase in the living room."

Stephanie didn't know what to say. She'd thought that Devi had guessed about her. She hadn't expected this.

Devi reached for her books.

"I'd better go. I said I'd be back for supper."

Stephanie found her voice.

"Is it a good book?"

"I don't know. I haven't read it."

"Oh."

"Have you?"

"I looked through it," said Stephanie, "a little bit."

"And?"

"It's ok I guess."

Devi stepped away from the table.

"Do you want to walk home with me? Or do you have to stay here?"

Stephanie pushed back her chair. She was suddenly glad about Devi being there. It had been a long afternoon.

"I'll walk back with you." She stood up. "It's good you saw me."

Devi smiled.

"Come on," she said. "Let's go."

CHAPTER TWELVE

The work on the dinosaur sculpture was almost finished. Plaster molds had been made for the bones and the sculpture was ready to be cast in concrete. Stephanie had spent Friday organizing a work party for the following day and on Saturday she met up with Eric, Devi and Anne Delaney over at Kate and Mary's house.

During the work on the dinosaur Stephanie and Kate had slowly taken over Mary's studio as their workshop. The walls were gradually filled with dinosaur diagrams and dimension charts. Bits of clay and books and models littered the rest of the room. It no longer resembled a painter's studio but an archaeological site.

Mary had relinquished her workplace with surprising willingness, telling them that she was in a slow period and that they could have it for as long as they wanted. Mary seemed almost too good-natured sometimes and Stephanie wondered if they were taking advantage of that good nature and should give her studio back. But they needed a large, bright room to work in and it suited all their purposes. Mary did seem to be in a "slow period"; wandering around the house and garden looking like she wanted to paint, but never actually doing it. She spent a lot of time staring off into space. Stephanie knew what that was like. She knew how hard it was to be constantly thinking of things and never being able, for one reason or another, to do anything about them.

Much to Stephanie's relief all her friends liked Kate Burton. She'd been afraid they might think it a little weird that she was friends with someone who was so much older than they all were. But because Kate was not of the same generation as their parents they didn't see her as any kind of threat and didn't object to her presence. In fact they all seemed to like her a lot and were a bit overawed by the amount of energy she possessed.

"She moves quicker than I do," Devi commented.

In fact the additional people had seemed to increase Kate's vitality. She sped around the proceedings, doing this, suggesting that. She was beginning to make Stephanie feel quite tired.

They had to fill the molds with concrete. Then the molds had to be left for two to three weeks, to give the concrete time to set properly. Stephanie and Kate had arranged for the molds to be moved to the sculpture site at the end of the concrete-setting period. The molds would be opened on site. Any small holes would be filled with concrete. Any rough spots would be sanded down. Then the sculpture would be waxed and assembled into its proper formation. As the concrete would make the different sections incredibly heavy they had to have the help of a hoist and the several people who would operate that hoist.

Pouring the concrete into the molds was a critical step in the process, but only Stephanie seemed to be concerned about it. Everyone else was relaxed and seemed not to notice that it was of such tremendous importance. Stephanie was glad that Mary was away for the day. She didn't know how kindly Mary would take to the extra activity and mess in her previously unspoilt studio. She hoped they could get everything cleaned up by the time she got home. She was glad also that Anne Delaney was working across the room from her. When she was anywhere nearby Stephanie found it impossible to concentrate.

Everyone seemed very impressed with the size of the molds and with the amount of concrete it took to fill them.

"You're not going to carry them out of here?" asked Devi. "They'll weigh a ton."

"No, no," Stephanie explained. "Some people are coming to move them. The school pays for all the stuff like that."

"Stuff like what?"

"All the stuff I can't do."

They worked solidly for most of the day, breaking only for a half hour lunch, which they ate on the floor of the studio, beside the tubs of liquid concrete and the molds. They had all brought different things for lunch and they shared the spoils so everyone could have a little of everything.

"This dinosaur's turning out alright." Devi took a bite of her sandwich.

"And," said Eric, "we get to put this work toward our art mark." Eric was all for being credited for his labours.

"Speaking of art," said Devi. "You know Mr. Hassam?" She had that dramatic "I can't help but tell" edge to her voice and Stephanie wondered what piece of gossip she was going to try and draw out for maximum effect.

"What about Mr. Hassam?" asked Stephanie impatiently.

"You know where he was on Friday night?"

"No."

"Guess where my brother saw him?"

"Pass the chips," said Eric.

Devi pushed the bowl roughly over to him.

"Where?" said Stephanie, tired of Devi's stories. She wondered sometimes if Devi really wanted to be gossipy like this, or if she simply couldn't help it. Maybe it was just a habit.

"My brother saw him going into a gay bar."

There was silence.

Stephanie was glad Kate was downstairs.

"Mr. Hassam's a queer?" Eric sounded surprised.

"A fag?" said Anne Delaney, equally incredulous.

Stephanie was certain her face was red and kept her eyes lowered to the floor.

"My brother was across the street and saw him going into the bar. He said he was positive it was Mr. Hassam. Positive." Devi drew the word out, syllable by syllable.

"He doesn't look like a fag," said Anne.

"This will turn me right off art," said Eric.

Stephanie didn't say anything. She felt almost sick. What if they ever found out about her? How could she ever hope to be herself in a world that would hate her for what she was? She couldn't look at Devi.

At this moment Kate appeared back upstairs. She must have heard something from the hallway. Her face looked a little flushed. Or maybe she was just out of breath from climbing the stairs.

"Come to think of it," said Anne, not seeming to notice or care about Kate's arrival. "I saw him over the Christmas break in a movie line up, and he was with a man then."

"And he once touched me on the arm," said Eric. "The left arm."

Stephanie kept her head down. She felt that as long as she didn't look at them they wouldn't know, but if they saw her face they'd guess her secret. She wanted to die.

"Now Eric." It was Kate speaking. She sounded stern. Stephanie had been right, she was angry.

"When he touched your arm what did he say? Did he make some sort of proposition?"

Stephanie raised her head a little and saw that Devi had a small smile on her face. Eric looked a bit red.

"No," he said faltering. "He, he said 'good work'. I'd done well on a project," he stopped. "I don't usually do well in art."

"So the touch wasn't meant in a sexual context?" said Kate.

"No."

"Is it really any of your business what he does when he's not at school?"

Stephanie lifted her head and looked at Eric and Anne. They seemed a little uncomfortable. She was slightly pleased.

"Yes, but it's not right," put in Anne. "It's sick."

"And why is it sick?"

"Because it's unnatural."

Stephanie couldn't look over at Anne. Why did it have to be her that was saying this? Why did she seem to be the one who minded the most? Anne. Anne Delaney, the person who consumed Stephanie's every thought.

"And why is it unnatural?" Kate didn't sound as irritated. In fact she almost sounded as if she were enjoying it. Maybe she'd been party to similar discussions before and was used to all this.

"Because it is."

"Why?"

"Because." It was obvious that Anne hadn't thought about it a great deal. All she'd done was accept the view that homosexuality was unnatural. She hadn't bothered to question it at all for herself. Stephanie realized that if Anne hadn't given it much thought then it was probably not a big part of her life and if so then it was very unlikely that she would ever reciprocate Stephanie's affection.

"Because," said Anne again. She was holding onto her half eaten sandwich so tightly that the bread was all dented under her fingers. "Because there have to be children."

Devi giggled and Stephanie held back what might have been a burst of hysterical laughter but which could just as easily have been a sob.

Kate smiled. "There will always be children. I'm not saying that the whole world should become gay, just that those people that are be accepted for who they are. Without condemnation," she added.

Anne didn't reply. Perhaps she couldn't think of a response.

Eric, who had been listening quite intently to Kate, said, "That's fair enough. But I won't feel the same way in art class now. Not after what I know about Mr. Hassam."

Stephanie saw a shadow pass over Kate's face. "It's no use," she thought. "They're not going to change their minds because they think they're right. And they think they're right because most people think that way."

Devi now seemed a little irritated by the way the conversation was going. She got impatiently to her feet.

"Let's finish this stuff," she said. "I have to be going soon."

Later that day Stephanie was working with Eric stirring the concrete to use on the rib bones when he suddenly stopped stirring and looked intently at her.

"Stephanie," he said, sounding very serious.

"Yes," she didn't look up.

"Would you like to go out with me again sometime?"

Stephanie felt her body go cold. She remembered the last time they'd gone out and how terrible it had all been. She looked across the room at Anne Delaney working industriously on the pelvic bone.

"Well," she said and then stopped. What could she say?

"Well," she said again.

"We could do anything you like," said Eric helpfully. "We could go to a movie. Or a concert. Or anywhere."

"I can't," said Stephanie. At least she could be honest. Even if she couldn't tell Anne Delaney how she felt about her she could tell Eric how she felt about him. It was important that she treat him fairly, that she was as honest as she felt she could be.

Eric looked startled.

"Why not?"

This was the hard part.

"I'm just not interested in you, like that. I mean, I like you. But I like you as a friend." She saw the look on Eric's face. "A very good friend. One of my best friends. Maybe one of the best friends I'll ever have."

Eric still looked upset.

"I'm sorry," said Stephanie. "Sometimes things just don't work out the way it seems they will. I can't help the way I feel. It's nobody's fault."

Eric had started stirring the concrete again.

"Well," he said.

"You're not mad. Are you?"

"No."

"Because it's not a thing to be mad about."

"I know."

Stephanie looked over at Anne Delaney again. She had sounded so hateful when she'd been talking about Mr. Hassam.

"Well," said Eric. "Would you like to go out sometime. As friends?"

"Sure."

Eric stopped stirring. "Ok. I think this is almost ready. Is it the plates next?"

"The plates," confirmed Stephanie and went to find the mold.

As she was separating the plate mold from the tangle of plaster on the workbench, she felt a hand on her shoulder.

"What about the children?" asked a plaintive voice.

Stephanie froze. It sounded like Anne Delaney. She turned quickly around and saw Devi standing behind her, grinning.

"Wasn't that just about the dumbest thing you ever heard?" said Devi in her normal voice.

"Well," said Stephanie weakly. "Maybe she was concerned."

"Come on." Devi knew when Stephanie was lying. They'd been friends a long time.

Stephanie smiled. "Yes," she said. "It was about the dumbest thing."

CHAPTER THIRTEEN

The night before the concrete casts were to be taken to the site to erect the sculpture Stephanie had dinner with Kate and Mary. It was a celebration dinner of sorts. They were celebrating their successful collaboration and the imminent conclusion of the project. They were celebrating the project itself. Stephanie was celebrating her new friends. Mary was probably celebrating the return of her studio.

They ate in Kate's and Mary's kitchen. Sitting at the wooden table with the lights turned off and several candles burning bravely in the dark. They had all made the meal – another collaborative effort and that made it all the more special a celebration.

"Here's to dinosaurs," said Kate when they were all seated and about to begin. She raised her glass.

"Here's to extinction," offered Mary, raising hers.

"Here's to bones," said Stephanie and they all touched glasses over the candle flames.

"God." Mary squinted through the semi-darkness. "What is it I'm eating? I can't see a thing. I think my eyes are going."

"Your eyes have gone, dear," said Kate kindly.

Stephanie suppressed a giggle.

Mary ignored both the comment and the choked back laughter.

"Are you going to celebrate again when the sculpture is erected?" Mary was still squinting. It made her look a little evil with the shadows gathering around her eyes.

"Sure," said Stephanie. She had a pleasant vision of endless celebration.

"And what's the next project?" asked Kate.

"The next project?"

"Don't sound so alarmed. Aren't you considering another one?" Stephanie looked down at her plate and stabbed at a potato with her fork.

"Maybe," she said. "Maybe I'd like to do another one. But I need a new idea first." She raised the forkful of potato towards her mouth and held it poised in front of her lips. "Do you think it would be ok to be both a paleontologist and a sculptor?"

"Of course," said Kate. "I think it would be a wonderful profession."

"Do you think it matters," Stephanie still held the potato just in front of her mouth, "if people think you're weird?"

"Are you weird?" asked Mary.

"Am I?" Stephanie asked Kate.

Kate didn't answer for a while. She was staring over Stephanie's shoulder at the wall behind her.

"Listen," she said finally. "When I studied paleontology it was during a time when very few women were becoming paleontologists and there was resistance. Mostly from my parents actually. But later it turned around and people respected me for doing what I wanted to do." She stopped looking at the wall and looked at Stephanie instead. "You're not responsible for what other people think of you. You're responsible for what you think of yourself. And in my experience the most important thing is to live your life in the way you want to live it."

"Being true to who you are," interjected Mary.

"But," Stephanie put her fork back down on the plate. It had started to get heavy. "It takes so long to figure out who you are."

"You're well on your way," said Kate. "You've done a remarkable job on this project. It's easy to have an idea. It's a lot harder to follow that idea through to the end."

"I sort of had no choice. I won that contest."

"Of course you had a choice."

"You did a remarkable job too," said Stephanie. "I wouldn't have been able to do it without you."

99

"It was fun." Kate smiled. "I enjoyed myself tremendously. And I'd certainly be willing to work with you again."

"But next time," said Mary. "We'll get you another workroom. My studio isn't really cut out to be a museum. Not that I minded," she added. "But on a permanent basis I'd prefer if you could work somewhere else."

"We could convert a part of the barn," suggested Kate. "We could build a sculpture studio out in the barn."

"Perfect," said Mary. "A project for the spring."

"Mary likes projects for the spring," Kate told Stephanie. "She gets restless for change when the warm weather comes."

"We could all do it." Stephanie was excited by the idea of another group effort. "And maybe my friends would help again."

"Yes," said Kate decisively. "A project for the spring."

"I'm sorry," said Mary. "But this can't go on."

"What can't go on?" asked Kate and Stephanie in unison.

"This darkness. I really can't see."

"Here." Stephanie moved the candles over toward Mary and arranged them around her plate.

All the light was suddenly transferred to Mary and her food, both being framed in the soft light of the candles. The effect was quite eerie.

"You look like you're about to be sacrificed," said Kate cheerfully.

"Thanks."

They lingered over the meal until the candles had shrunk themselves down to a flicker and a puddle of wax.

They were having tea and were all feeling very comfortable and relaxed. Stephanie leaned over her mug towards Kate and Mary.

"Can I ask you something?"

"Go ahead," said Mary.

Stephanie didn't say anything for a moment.

"What's it like," she stopped and started again. "What's it like living together for so long?"

"Has it been long?" Kate looked at Mary. "Well I guess it has. It's seemed awfully short actually."

"It's seemed long to me," said Mary, and smiled which in the dull light of the candles looked more like a grimace.

"How did you meet?" Stephanie, her elbows on the table, leaned further forward, over the dying candles.

"At the university," replied Mary. "I was a brilliant

art student in my final year and Kate was an assistant professor of paleontology."

"I thought she was conceited," confided Kate. "But I liked her paintings."

"And I thought she had good artistic judgement but was a lousy judge of character." Mary took a long sip of her tea.

"Sometimes it's been serious, but mostly it's been fun."

"A lot of fun," agreed Kate.

Stephanie sat back a little in her chair. All the unasked and unanswered questions lay between them on the table. It was assumed, she thought, that those questions didn't need to be asked, that something was understood.

"What's it like?" she said again. "Living together for so long."

"You just asked that." Kate looked a little puzzled.

Stephanie didn't know how to say it. She played with the candle wax for a moment before trying again.

"I've been upstairs," she said hopelessly.

"Yes you have," agreed Kate. "Many times."

"I've seen all the rooms upstairs."

"Yes."

"Oh," put in Mary suddenly. "She's talking about our secret." From the way she was smiling Stephanie gathered that it wasn't much of a secret.

"Yes," she said with relief. "That's what I'm talking about."

"Well," said Kate, "we already told you what it was like being together for all these years."

"No, no." Mary put a hand gently on Kate's arm. "She doesn't care about that really. She wants to know what it's like being a lesbian for all these years. It's the lesbian part of this relationship she's interested in, not the relationship part."

Stephanie didn't know if she would have put it quite like that, but there was truth in what Mary said.

"Maybe it's rude to ask such personal questions," said Stephanie apologetically. "I don't mean to be rude. I...."

"It's alright." Kate smiled reassuringly. "We're not bothered. Part of getting to know people is asking questions."

Stephanie leaned back a little in her chair, took a sip of tea. It had finally happened. She could finally talk about herself, about Anne Delaney, about all that confusion and panic inside herself. Having kept it bottled up for so long though she found it hard to shape her feelings into words and offer them up to the expectant faces of Kate and Mary. She decided to try and be as simple as possible.

"I think I'm in love with a girl," she said.

"How wonderful," exclaimed Mary.

"Not really."

"Does she love you back?" asked Kate.

"No. She doesn't know how I feel." Stephanie put her mug down on the table. "I don't know how I feel."

"You're in love," said Mary cheerfully.

"I think so. But," said Stephanie, "I've never been in love before so how do I really know? And if I am, what does that mean?"

"Does it have to mean something beyond what it is?" Kate frowned slightly. "Isn't love enough?"

"A question asked many times through the ages," interjected Mary. "Is love enough? Is money enough? Is anything enough?"

"Ok," said Stephanie. "Suppose I am in love with this person." She couldn't bring herself to say Anne's name, it would destroy the objectivity she was trying to maintain. "Suppose I am in love. Does this mean that I'm gay?"

There was a silence.

"I don't know," said Kate. "It's considered

'natural' for girls to get crushes on other girls."

"It's also considered 'natural' for them to stop," added Mary. "Maybe you'll just have to wait and see what happens. Give it some time."

"If you are gay," continued Kate, "then sooner or later you'll know for sure. You'll be attracted to someone who's attracted to you. You'll know."

"Does it worry you?" Mary squinted through the half-darkness to get a better focus on Stephanie.

"Most of the time," said Stephanie. "Everybody seems to think it's so terrible."

"I don't," said Mary.

"I don't either," said Kate.

Stephanie smiled. She felt relaxed and secure in this house with her new friends.

"Maybe I don't think it is either," she said.

CHAPTER FOURTEEN

Snow had been forecast for the day the sculpture was to be erected. But that morning, when they all assembled at the school waiting for the trucks to bring the concrete molds there was no snow. The sky was a dull grey. The air was so cold they could see their breaths. But no snow.

They huddled together by the front steps – Stephanie, Kate, Mary, Eric, Mark and Devi. Anne Delaney, much to Stephanie's relief, hadn't been able to make it that morning. She'd had to go with her parents somewhere. They'd forced her to go, she'd said bitterly over the phone to Stephanie. Something about a sick relation. Stephanie hadn't been able to concentrate very well when talking to Anne. The mere sound of her voice sent Stephanie spinning out of control.

The morning hadn't started off very well. The weather was supposed to have been a lot warmer but at the last minute some gigantic cold front had moved into the region and plummeted the temperature. The trucks bringing the concrete casts were supposed to have arrived at the site by 9:00. It was now 10:30. Stephanie herself didn't get there until 9:45 because her parents' car wouldn't start and they'd had to get a jump start from a neighbour. On top of all this she was incredibly anxious that the sculpture itself would look terrible when all the pieces were finally assembled. She'd lain awake most of the night worrying about how stupid it would look. All in all it was not, so far, the best of days.

"Where are they?" asked Stephanie impatiently, for perhaps the sixteenth time.

Nobody replied. Nobody had an answer.

"I'm freezing." Mark shoved his hands further into his parka pockets. "Why is it so cold?"

"It was supposed to snow. At least it's not doing that." Mary tried to lighten the mood.

"Shut up, dear," said Kate, adding the "dear" after quite a considerable pause. Stephanie giggled. Mary surrendered her cheerful facade and collapsed into the companionable gloom. They stood there in silence. Heads down. Hands in pockets.

There was a sound above all the other sounds that filled the corner of the schoolyard where they stood. The sound of large engines. Stephanie turned and saw three trucks making their way over the pavement towards them.

"They're here," she said, quite needlessly for by that time everyone had seen them as well.

Things improved. The pieces of the sculpture were gently lifted from the trucks. The molds were removed and the pieces were put into place by the cranes on the trucks. Everyone stopped complaining about the cold and watched eagerly as the sculpture took shape.

"What if they drop something?" said Stephanie nervously as the dinosaur pelvis swung over her head.

"They won't," said Kate.

"But what if they do?"

"They won't."

"And what if it's no good? What if it looks stupid when it's all together?"

Kate laid her hand on Stephanie's shoulder.

"Stop it," she said gently. "It's too late for thinking like that. It's too late. It's done."

Stephanie stopped. They stood together and watched the sculpture become itself.

When it was completely up and the trucks had left Stephanie and her friends went over the entire piece, inspecting it for imperfections and repairing the few rough spots in the concrete. After that they waxed it, as protection from the weather. And then it was finished. It was over. A huge skull set against the flatness of the school grounds. A huge, beautiful dinosaur head. Stephanie still felt so nervous and anxious that she couldn't take it all in that present moment. The whole day seemed unreal, seemed to exist somewhere else. She couldn't really believe that it was over, that her work was finished.

They all went back to Stephanie's house for food and hot drinks. It was intended to have been a celebration but no one seemed all that happy. Everyone was let down now that the project was finished.

"It's just," said Devi, "it's just kind of depressing more than anything else. I mean, it's good it's all together. And it looks great. But it's – well, it's over."

"Yes," echoed Eric. "Now there's nothing for us to do."

"You can admire it," suggested Mary.

"How long does admiring last? A week? Maybe two weeks?"

Stephanie looked around the room at this group of her friends and family and felt happy again.

"In the spring," she said, "I think I'm going to build something else. Something else that's big."

With this announcement, the mood changed and the gathering slowly became the celebration that it was intended to be. They spent several hours talking and eating and planning the next project.

Later, as Stephanie was going to the hall closet to get the coats for the people who were leaving she saw Anne Delaney standing outside on the front steps. She opened the door.

"I was just going to knock," said Anne.

"I was just going to get the coats," said Stephanie. She opened the door wider and Anne stepped into the front hall.

"I managed to get away early." Anne made no move to take off her coat. "I thought you might all be here."

Stephanie sat down on a stair. "Everyone's in the living room."

"I can't stay." Anne leaned against the door. "Parents."

Stephanie thought that Anne's parents must be stricter than her own to keep such tight control over her time. She felt a rush of gratefulness for all the times her parents had let her do what she wanted.

"Anyway," said Anne. "I only came to tell you that I went past the sculpture on the bus over here and it looks good. No, it looks great."

"Thanks." Stephanie suddenly realized that she was talking to Anne Delaney and that she wasn't saying anything stupid. It was fine. Maybe she was so exhausted from the morning's ordeal that nothing affected her. Or maybe she was used to Anne Delaney being around and it wasn't such a big deal to talk to her now. She also realized that during the raising of the sculpture she hadn't thought of Anne once. Not once. Maybe that little absence from Stephanie's thoughts had made a difference.

"Is that what you're going to do?" asked Anne.

"What?"

"With your life."

"My life?"

Anne put her hands in the pocket of her coat.

"Is this what you want to do? Make things out of bones."

"I think so."

"What about money?"

"I don't know." Stephanie had never thought about it in those terms before. "I expect it will be alright."

"It's quite a brave thing to do."

Stephanie looked in confusion at Anne. It had never seemed to her to be the least bit brave. What was she talking about? It occurred to Stephanie that she didn't know very much about Anne Delaney; and the things she did know were things she didn't care for.

"What do you want to do?" she asked.

Anne hesitated before replying and then turned to Stephanie with a big smile on her face.

"I want to be rich."

"What else?"

The smile disappeared.

"Nothing else."

"How are you going to get rich?"

"I don't know."

"Well I don't think it's that easy to get rich," said Stephanie doubtfully. She wanted to add "or that exciting," but stopped herself. Money was something she knew was necessary but she didn't think it would be interesting to spend a lifetime trying to accumulate large amounts of it.

There was a silence.

Anne took her hands out of her pockets.

"I'd better go. My parents will be waiting."

Stephanie stood up and opened the door for her.

"See you," said Anne.

"See you." Stephanie closed the door.

Stephanie stood by the front door and peered through the window at Anne walking down the driveway and out onto the street.

"I thought you were getting my coat?" Devi was

standing behind her looking over her shoulder through the glass to see what she was staring at. Stephanie turned to her friend.

"You know what Anne Delaney wants to do with her life?"

"What?"

"Get rich."

"What else?"

Stephanie smiled. "That's what I thought, what else? Nothing else."

"Maybe she just hasn't figured it out yet." Devi liked to be able to find reasons for everyone's behaviour.

"No, I think that's what she wants to do." Stephanie glanced toward the door again. "I mean it's an ok thing to do, if that's what you want. But it just seems so different from my life."

"I never knew why you wanted Anne Delaney to help anyway," said Devi. "She's not your friend or anything."

"Well," thought Stephanie. "I could tell her or I couldn't tell her." Devi, aggravating as she some-times could be, was still Stephanie's oldest friend.

"Can you keep a secret?"

"You know I can't." Devi looked distressed. "I blab everything."

"This is a personal thing." Stephanie took a deep breath and let it out slowly. "I wouldn't want anyone else to know."

"I could try." Devi looked doubtful. "Ok, I could try hard."

"You could promise."

"Alright, I promise."

"You really promise?"

"I really promise."

Stephanie took a deep breath.

"Remember at the library? The books I had on the table?"

"Yes?"

"I was reading them."

"So?"

"I like Anne Delaney."

"So?"

This wasn't going very well. Stephanie thought that would be all she'd need to say. Maybe she should forget about it. Backtrack her way out of it. Lie. Change the topic.

"I like – well actually I don't think I do so much anymore – but anyway." She paused and tried again. "I liked Anne Delaney the way you like Eric."

"How do you know I like Eric?" Devi looked a little startled. Stephanie waited for her to get over the fact that her infatuation with Eric was obvious. It didn't take very long.

"You mean," said Devi, a little too loudly. "You mean you're gay?"

"Maybe." Stephanie suddenly felt defensive and wished she hadn't said anything. "I don't really know. I did like Anne Delaney. What if I am?"

"You have nothing in common with Anne Delaney. I could have told you that." Devi seemed confused by Stephanie's revelation. "You could have asked me."

Stephanie leaned against the door. "I didn't know what to say. It's hard. Do you hate me?"

Devi smiled at her feet.

"You know when I said that my brother saw Mr. Hassam in that gay bar?"

"Yes."

"Well he didn't see him from across the street. He saw him inside the bar. That's how I knew for sure he was there."

"Your brother's gay?" This was the last thing Stephanie had expected Devi to be telling her.

"He told me about a year ago."

"And you never told me?" Devi, who couldn't keep a secret, who enjoyed spreading gossip more than anyone hadn't told Stephanie this piece of information. It was hard for Stephanie to believe that Devi could be so restrained.

"I thought you wouldn't understand," said Devi.

"And I thought you wouldn't understand about me." Stephanie smiled. "Don't go yet. Stay for a while."

Devi smiled back. "Let's go upstairs. I can hear someone arguing. I want to know what they're talking about."

At the top of the stairs she turned to see if Stephanie was following. Stephanie wasn't. She was still standing by the front door.

"Come on."

Stephanie started up the stairs. Devi waited for her.

"There's just one thing I don't understand," Devi said.

"What?" Stephanie felt herself grow cold with apprehension.

"What?"

"Why Anne Delaney? She's sort of a jerk."

Stephanie smiled, and then, out of relief more than anything, began to laugh. When they went back into the living room they were both laughing.

The group in the living room didn't seem to have missed Stephanie at all. Mark and Kate were talking about education. Stephanie's mother was telling Eric something about a car she'd once owned. And, Stephanie noted with pleasure, her father and Mary were engaged in an animated discussion of colour reproduction. Maybe now that he'd met gay people, now that he'd talked to them and found he liked them, he'd stop being so narrow-minded in his opinions.

"It's been a good day," said Devi, "hasn't it?"

Stephanie turned and smiled at her.

"Yes, it has."

The following morning Stephanie left the house quietly before sunrise. The streets were snow covered, her footsteps sounded heavy and soft on the sidewalk leading to school. All night long she'd dreamt that the sculpture didn't really exist, that the entire project was an illusion. She'd woken early. She had to see for herself that it was real.

The sun was prying up a corner of sky as she entered the yard. Ahead of her, beyond a snowy stretch of ground, rising out of the earth like a mountain, was the sculpture. Stephanie stopped. So incredibly large. So beautiful. The sun crept through the shapes, laying fingers of light on the stone. Stephanie walked over to the sculpture and put her mittened hand on a dinosaur leg bone. She took her hand away, took off the mitten and placed her bare hand on the surface. Cold, a little rough. While she had her hand on it it belonged to her. If she lifted her hand away it wouldn't be hers anymore. It would belong to itself and become part of the space around it.

The sun was sweeping light through the stones. Stephanie took her hand away.